THIS RISING MOON
BOOK BELONGS TO:

_____

THE SEED AND THE GIANT SAGUARO

by **JENNIFER WARD**

illustrated by **MIKE K. RANGNER**

rising moon

www.risingmoonbooks.com

Composed in the United States of America
Printed in China

Edited by Theresa Howell
Designed by David Jenney & Katie Jennings
Production supervised by Donna Boyd

FIRST IMPRESSION 2003
ISBN-13: 978-0-87358-845-4
ISBN-10: 0-87358-845-2

05   06   07   5   4   3

Library of Congress Cataloging-in-Publication Data

Ward, Jennifer, 1963-
The seed and the giant saguaro / by Jennifer Ward ; illustrated by Mike Rangner.
p. cm.
Summary: A packrat, carrying fruit from the giant saguaro, is chased by various desert
animals and inadvertently helps spread the cactus's seed. Includes information on saguaros.
[1. Saguaro—Fiction. 2. Cactus—Fiction. 3. Desert animals—Fiction. 4. Desert
ecology—Fiction. 5. Ecology—Fiction. 6. Stories in rhyme.] I. Rangner, Mike, ill. II. Title.

PZ8.3.W2135Se2003   [E]—dc21

2003046578

For my parents.
Paul and Charlene Sultan.
with love.
— J.W.

To my
wonderful wife Theresa
and my two great kids.
Heather and Thomas
— M. K. R.

This is the giant saguaro.

This is the fruit

That grew on the giant saguaro.

This is the pack rat that ran in a hurry

And carried the fruit with a great deal of worry

That grew on the giant saguaro.

This is the snake that slid with no sound

That trailed the pack rat that ran in a hurry

And carried the fruit with a great deal of worry

That grew on the giant saguaro.

This is the bird that raced

on the ground

That chased the snake that slid with no sound

That trailed the pack rat that ran in a hurry

And carried the fruit with a great deal of worry

That grew on the giant saguaro.

Here's the coyote that quickly dashed

That followed the bird that raced on the ground

That chased the snake that slid with no sound

That trailed the pack rat that ran in a hurry

And carried the fruit with a great deal of worry

That grew on the giant saguaro.

These are the clouds that rumbled and flashed

Above the coyote that quickly dashed

That followed the bird that raced on the ground

That chased the snake that slid with no sound

That trailed the pack rat that ran in a hurry

And carried the fruit with a great deal of worry

That grew on the giant saguaro.

This is the rain that tumbled down

That came from the clouds that rumbled and flashed

Above the coyote that quickly dashed

That followed the bird that raced on the ground

That chased the snake that slid with no sound

That trailed the pack rat that ran in a hurry

And carried the fruit with a great deal of worry

That grew on the giant saguaro.

This is the earth, all moist and brown

Soaked by the rain that tumbled down

That poured from the clouds that rumbled and flashed

Above the coyote that quickly dashed

That followed the bird that raced on the ground

That chased the snake that slid with no sound

That trailed the pack rat that ran in a hurry

And carried the fruit with a great deal of worry

That grew on the giant saguaro.

These are the seeds so black and tiny

That sunk in the earth, all moist and brown

Soaked by the rain that tumbled down

That poured from the clouds that rumbled and flashed

Above the coyote that quickly dashed

That followed the bird that raced on the ground

That chased the snake that slid with no sound

That trailed the pack rat that ran in a hurry

And carried the fruit with a great deal of worry

That grew on the giant saguaro.

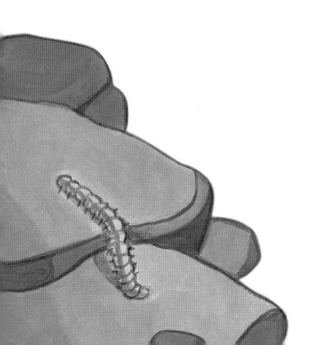

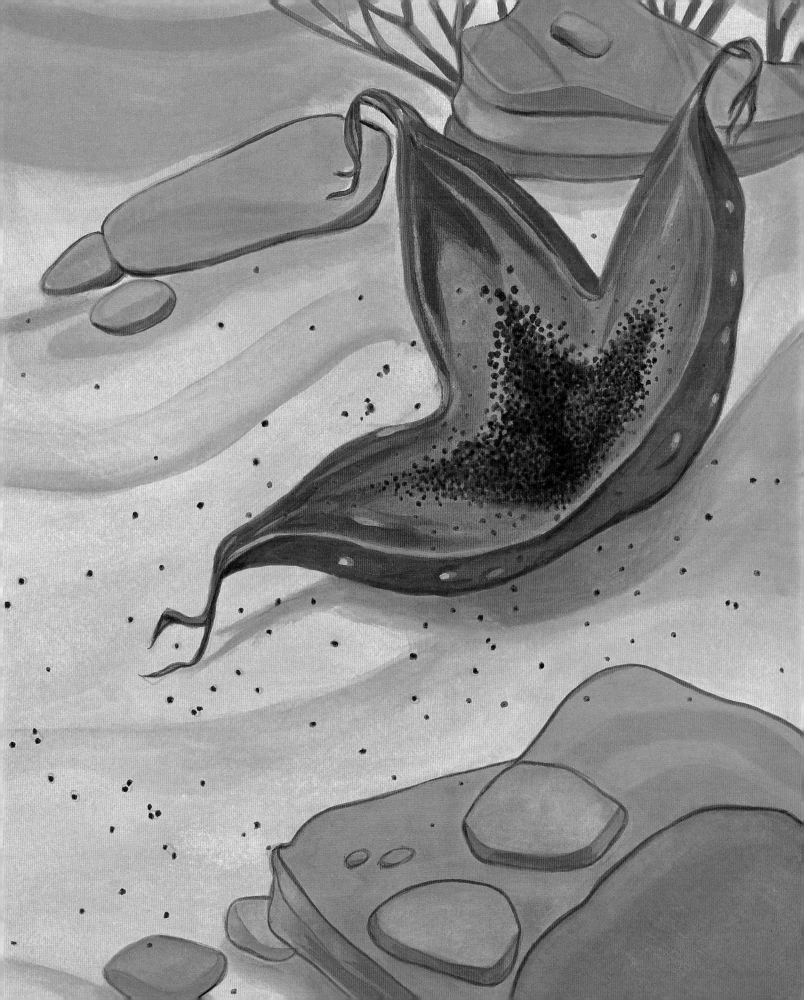

And this is the cactus, new and spiny

That grew from a seed so black and tiny

Because of the pack rat that stole the fruit

That dropped the seed that slowly took root...

And grew to a

giant saguaro.

SENSATIONAL SAGUAROS

Imagine you are ten years old, but only as tall as a finger on your hand. Well, that's how tall you would be if you were a ten-year-old saguaro cactus. The saguaro (pronounced suh-wah-roh) only grows in the Sonoran Desert of southwest North America, where the weather is hot and dry.

The saguaro may start out small, but it can grow very tall. After one hundred fifty years, a saguaro might be fifty feet tall—that's taller than two full-grown giraffes! You might say the saguaro is slow to grow! And let's not forget the amazing arms on the saguaro cactus. A saguaro might spend much of its life without any arms at all because most saguaros don't begin sprouting and growing arms until they are seventy years old.

In the months of May and June, saguaros grow white, waxy flowers at their tops and on the tips of their arms. Then, just in time for the rainy season, a green fruit will grow where the flower once was. As it ripens, the fruit turns bright red and splits open to show its 2,000 to 4,000 seeds. Of all those thousands of seeds, only one or two might grow to become a new saguaro.

The saguaro trunk has pleats that can swell and shrink like an accordion, depending on how much rain it absorbs. The saguaro can soak up hundreds of gallons of water during heavy rains — that's as much as seven bathtubs full of water!

The saguaro blossom is the state flower of Arizona.

The spines on the saguaro create shade from the sun, protect it, and help guide water down its ridges.

The saguaro has a shallow root system that spreads out over a large area.

TIMELINE

10 YEARS	20 YEARS	35 YEARS
2 inches tall	1 1/2 feet tall	6 feet tall

A full-grown saguaro can weigh 18,000 pounds (9 tons). That's heavier than a full-grown elephant!

The saguaro is home to many different kinds of animals, such as woodpeckers, owls, and pack rats.

The saguaro has waxy skin like a candle. This helps keep water stored inside.

The inside of the saguaro has a trunk made of wooden ribs.

70 YEARS

15 feet tall

100 YEARS

20 feet tall

150 YEARS

30 or more feet tall

FUN FACTS

Omnivore — An animal that eats both plants and animals is called an omnivore. Coyotes and roadrunners are omnivores because they eat small animals as well as plants.

Carnivore — An animal that eats other animals is called a carnivore. Rattlesnakes are carnivores. They eat small animals, such as mice and rats.

Herbivore — An animal that eats only plants is called an herbivore. Pack rats, deer, and rabbits are examples of herbivores.

Roadrunner — This bird spends most of its time on the ground, where it likes to hunt and eat lizards, insects, scorpions, other birds, and bird eggs. It is also cuckoo for rattlesnakes! The roadrunner is able to hunt and kill rattlesnakes because of its quick speed. It can run up to 17 miles per hour!

Coyote — Coyotes are members of the dog family. They can "dash" up to 30 miles per hour. They eat just about anything, from cactus and crickets to rodents and rabbits.

Rattlesnake — All rattlesnakes are poisonous and have a rattle at the tip of their body. The rattle is used to warn predators. "Watch out! I have a poisonous bite!" Each time a rattlesnake sheds its skin, a new section of rattle appears. A rattlesnake may shed its skin three times a year. Rattlesnakes eat lizards and small rodents, flicking out their tongues to "taste" the air and find prey.

Pack rat — Also known as the wood rat, the pack rat gets its name because it gathers items to build its nest, or midden. Sometimes, while carrying one item, a pack rat might come across something it likes better. Then, it drops the item it was carrying and picks up the new item to take back to its midden.